Where Do You Sleep, Little One?

Where Do You Sleep, Little One?

BY PATRICIA HOOPER

ILLUSTRATED BY JOHN WINCH

HOLIDAY HOUSE / New York

Little chipmunk, digging deep
In the yard, where do you sleep?

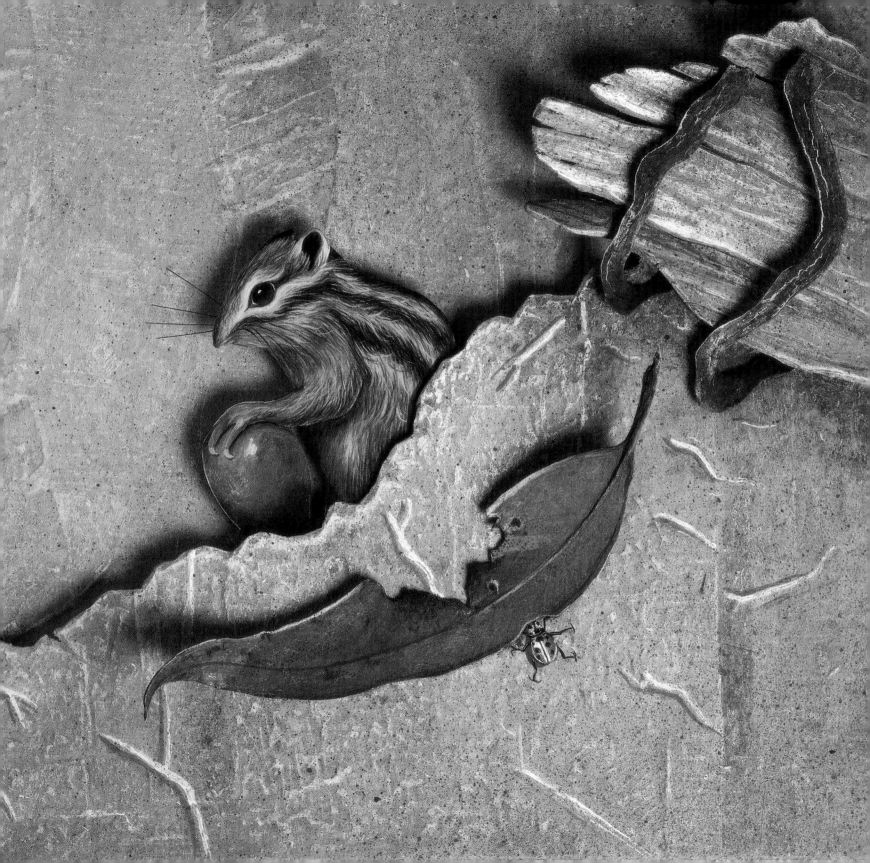

Underneath the roots and loam,
I follow many hallways home.

Little field mouse, gray and shy,
Where are you when owls fly?

I have made myself a bed
Of leaves and bark, as soft as bread.

Little fawn who ventures near,
Where are you when stars appear?

In the forest, dark and warm,
I can slumber, far from harm.

Little wren who's left the nest,
Will you find a place to rest?

In the shelter of a tree,
Sleep will come to comfort me.

Little rabbit in the snow,
Night is near, and you must go.

Deep in thickets, safe inside
Tangled hedges, I'll abide.

Little spider on the wall,
Tell me, do you sleep at all?

When the stars light up the skies,
I weave a cradle, just my size.

Little pony, goat, and sheep,
What warm bed does someone keep
Filled with straw so you can sleep?

In our stable dreams are deep,
Little child. Now, go to sleep.

For Jacob and Courtney
P. H.

For Madeleine, Martina, and Jessie
J. W.

Text copyright © 2001 by Patricia Hooper
Illustrations copyright © 2001 by John Winch
Photography by Ian Percival
All Rights Reserved
Printed in the United States of America
The medium for the artwork is oil on prepared
French handmade Arches paper.
The animals were cut out, arranged in layers,
and then photographed
against embossed backgrounds.
The text typeface is Galliard.
www.holidayhouse.com
First Edition

Library of Congress Cataloging-in-Publication Data
Hooper, Patricia, 1941–
Where do you sleep, little one? / by Patricia Hooper;
illustrated by John Winch.—1st ed.
p. cm.
ISBN 0-8234-1668-2 (hardcover)
1. Sleep—Juvenile poetry.
2. Animals—Juvenile poetry.
3. Children's poetry, American.
[1. Sleep—Poetry. 2. Animals—Poetry.
3. American poetry.]
I. Winch, John, 1944– ill. II. Title.
PS3558.O59 W47 2001
811'.54—dc21 00-053543

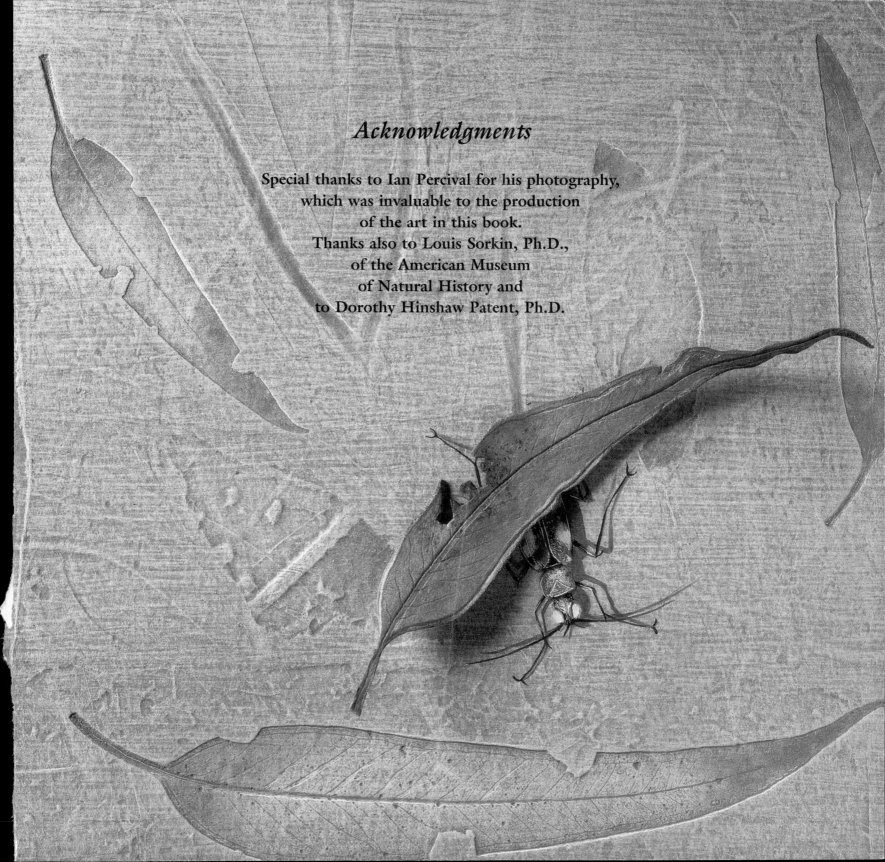

Acknowledgments

Special thanks to Ian Percival for his photography,
which was invaluable to the production
of the art in this book.
Thanks also to Louis Sorkin, Ph.D.,
of the American Museum
of Natural History and
to Dorothy Hinshaw Patent, Ph.D.